# DOLPHIN ISLAND

## A Daring Rescue

## A Daring Rescue

by Catherine Hapka
illustrated by Petur Antonsson

SCHOLASTIC INC.

Text copyright © 2019 by Catherine Hapka
Illustrations by Petur Antonsson, copyright © 2019 Scholastic Inc.

All rights reserved. Published by Scholastic Inc., *Publishers since 1920.* SCHOLASTIC and associated logos are trademarks and/or registered trademarks of Scholastic Inc.

The publisher does not have any control over and does not assume any responsibility for author or third-party websites or their content.

This book is a work of fiction. Names, characters, places, and incidents are either the product of the author's imagination or are used fictitiously, and any resemblance to actual persons, living or dead, business establishments, events, or locales is entirely coincidental.

ISBN 978-1-338-29018-9

10 9 8 7 6 5 4 3 2 1      19 20 21 22 23

Printed in U.S.A.      40
First printing 2019

Book design by Lizzy Yoder

# I
# Island Girl

"Look, Abby! Dolphins!"

"Where?" Abby Feingold raced over to her stepmother, Rachel, who was standing with her bare feet in the surf. It was a beautiful, hot, sunny summer day in the Florida Keys. Abby and Rachel were on the beach looking out across the peaceful lagoon at the sea between their island and Key West.

Yes, *their* island. Abby still could hardly believe that her family owned an island now! It had happened a few months ago when Daddy and Rachel got married.

Rachel's great-aunt Susan had given them this island, which was called Barnaby Key, as a wedding gift. Great-Aunt Susan had lived there for many years, and Rachel had loved visiting when she was Abby's age. But for the past ten years, Great-Aunt Susan had lived with her son in Miami, and nobody had lived on the island.

"Where are the dolphins?" Abby squinted to see past the sunlight glinting off the waves. Then she gasped. "Oh, I see them now!"

She held her breath and watched the dolphins. There were four or five of them—it was hard to tell, since they never stayed still. They leaped out of the water one after the other, seeming to play tag.

"They're beautiful, aren't they?" Rachel said. "I love dolphins."

"Me too." Abby smiled up at her new stepmother. Daddy always said that Rachel was the best thing to happen to him since Abby was born. Abby had to agree. She already couldn't imagine their family without her. Rachel was kind and smart and always smiling. Her father was from Jamaica, and Rachel had lived there until she was a little older than Abby was now. Rachel's voice still had a lilting accent that sounded like everything she said was a song.

Then Abby returned her gaze to the dolphins. She watched them jump and twist and play. One of the dolphins was a little smaller than the others. It leaped right over a bigger dolphin, then popped back up, seeming to laugh.

"I hope Daddy gets back in time to see the dolphins," Abby said, pushing aside a strand of wavy brown hair that the sea breeze had blown into her face.

"That would be nice," Rachel agreed. "I bet our guests would love seeing dolphins, too. Maybe we can add a dolphin-spotting boat trip to the schedule. What do you think?"

"That's a great idea." Abby took out her phone and

made a note of it. She'd received the phone for her eighth birthday, which had happened a few weeks after the wedding. Daddy said she was the most responsible just-turned-eight-year-old he knew, and that she deserved to have her own phone. Besides, living on an island, she might need it.

Next, Abby took a few photos of the dolphins. But they were pretty far away—when she looked at the photos, the dolphins looked like tiny gray dots.

"Oh well," she said. She stuck the phone back in the pocket of her shorts. "Maybe they'll come closer to the beach sometime."

"Maybe," Rachel agreed. "Anyway, I'm glad we saw them. I've always thought they were good luck. Maybe seeing them is a good sign for our brand-new resort!"

"I bet it is." Abby smiled. It was hard to believe that their island resort was finally open for business! The three of them had moved in soon after the wedding. Daddy had given up his job as a landscaper, and Rachel had told the school where she taught that she wouldn't be back in the fall.

The whole family had spent just about every second since then hard at work. They'd cleaned up and painted the rambling old main house and the six smaller guest bungalows. They'd raked seaweed and other debris off the narrow strip of white sand beach. And they'd cut back the jungle of vines and weeds growing over everything. Rachel and Abby had gone to Key West, a much bigger island that was about three miles away by boat, to pick out bed linens and other stuff to decorate the guest rooms. Daddy had spent hours planting beautiful tropical flowers and shrubs. Most of the plants had come from Key West and other nearby islands. A few had to be shipped in from the mainland, which was more than sixty miles away.

Now everything looked perfect. Abby knew their first group of guests was sure to love it!

Abby scanned the horizon, looking for the *Kismet*.

That was the name of the family's boat. They planned to use it to pick up guests from the Key West airport and to take them out fishing and scuba diving on the coral reefs.

Then she looked for the dolphins again. They were getting farther away. A second later, they disappeared around the rocky curve of shore at the far end of the beach.

Abby wished they could have stayed longer. But she reminded herself that she lived on an island now—not in their old apartment on the mainland, miles and miles from the beach. She would have plenty of chances to see dolphins and all kinds of other cool creatures.

Just then she saw movement out on the water. "There's the *Kismet*!" she cried, pointing. "The boat is coming back!"

# 2

# Welcome Party

Abby waved as the boat came closer. Then she and Rachel hurried over to the dock, which jutted out into the deep water near the house. By the time they got there, Daddy was jumping out to tie up the boat.

"Welcome to Barnaby Key!" Rachel called out to his passengers.

"Thank you," a young, pretty woman called back.

"Happy to be here!" added a cheerful-looking older man with a shiny bald head.

There were five other guests in the boat. Abby smiled

when she saw that one of them was a girl about her age. The girl had a pointy chin, big brown eyes, and freckles across her nose. Her wavy dark hair was held back by a sparkly headband.

Daddy helped all the guests out of the boat. The adults were already oohing and aahing over the clear water and flowers and palm trees.

Abby stepped forward to greet the girl. "Hi, I'm Abby," she said. "I'm eight. How old are you?"

"I'm seven, but I turn eight in August." The other girl smiled shyly. "My name is Bella."

"That's a pretty name," Abby said. "Where do you live?"

Bella pointed back the way the boat had come. "On Stock Island. That's right next to Key West."

"Really?" Abby was surprised. She'd expected most of the resort's guests to come from farther away. "Why'd you decide to come here?"

"My aunt and uncle are visiting from Virginia." Bella waved a hand toward the bald man and a petite dark-haired woman. "They wanted to relax somewhere quiet. So this place sounded perfect."

"Oh, it is!" Abby pointed toward the beach. "They can sit there all day long if they want to!"

Bella giggled. "They'll like that. So you live here on this little island?"

"Uh-huh." Abby shrugged. "Only for the past month or so, though. I used to live on the mainland." She told Bella about Great-Aunt Susan.

"Wow." Bella didn't say anything else, but she smiled again. Abby could tell that Bella was a little shy. But that was okay.

"Come on," Abby said. "I'll help carry your stuff to your bungalow. Then I'll give you a tour if you want."

"Sure, thanks." Bella picked up her backpack and followed Abby toward the end of the dock. The adults were already heading that way, too.

"The waves are really gentle on the beach," Abby told Bella. "So it's a good place to look for shells and sand crabs and stuff. The rest of the shoreline is mostly kind of rocky, except for the far end where there are mangroves. Oh! And guess what! I saw dolphins right out beyond the lagoon just now!"

"Really?" Bella looked excited. "I love dolphins! I always look for them when I'm at the beach."

"I love them, too. They're probably my favorite animal," Abby said. "There are tons of other animals here on the island, though, too. So far I've seen rabbits, turtles, a raccoon, a couple of iguanas, some other lizards I don't know the name of, and lots of different birds and fish." She shrugged. "Daddy says there might even be Key deer here, but we haven't seen any yet."

"Wow. How big is the island?" Bella asked.

"It's almost thirty acres. But only about five are cleared so far." Abby gestured to the forest beyond the dock. "We're going to clear a little more when we have time so we can plant more fruit trees and maybe a vegetable garden. But Daddy wants to keep most of the

island wild. We'll probably cut some paths for hiking, though."

She pointed out the main house, where she and Daddy and Rachel lived on the third floor. The open-air dining pavilion was nearby, with white sand-and-shell paths connecting it to the house and bungalows. Daddy had worked hard on the landscaping, planting colorful flowers and native grasses. Tall palm trees swayed over the beach and gardens.

Soon Abby and her parents had showed all the guests to their bungalows. Bella and her parents were in the Silver Palm Bungalow, which had two bedrooms. Her aunt and uncle were in the Moonflower Bungalow right next door. The young, pretty woman turned out to be a newlywed named Mrs. Smith-Patel. She and her new husband, Mr. Smith-Patel, were in the Orchid Bungalow at the far end of the beach.

"I like the names of the cabins," Bella said as she and Abby left the Silver Palm Bungalow.

"Thanks. It was my dad's idea to name them after plants," Abby told her. "He used to be a landscaper."

Bella nodded and looked around. "How many cabins are there?"

"Six," Abby said. "Plus three guest suites in the main house."

"Wow, that's a lot," Bella said. "Are we the only guests? The seven of us from the boat, I mean."

"Yes, for now." For a second, Abby felt worried. She'd been so excited about having guests that she hadn't thought about the number of guests they had. Only three bungalows were filled. That wasn't very many.

"Are those kayaks?" Bella pointed to a rack of colorful boats near the beach.

"Yes." Abby forgot about her worry. "It's really fun to kayak through the mangroves. Want to try it?"

"Sure! Maybe we'll see some dolphins, or at least some other cool wildlife." Bella smiled. "Let's go!"

# 3

## Old and New Friends

An hour before bedtime that night, Abby knocked on the open office door. The office was a small room tucked under the stairs on the first floor. It was where Daddy and Rachel kept all the important paperwork for the new resort. Daddy was in there sitting at the computer.

"Hi," Abby said. "Happy end of the first day of business!"

Daddy chuckled and ran a hand over his head, making tufts of dark hair stick up. "Thanks, Abs. It was a good day, wasn't it?"

"It sure was," she agreed. "Can I email Layla? I want to tell her all about it."

"Of course." Daddy stood up so Abby could take his place at the computer. "Don't be long, though. It's getting late, and we have a big day planned for our guests tomorrow."

Abby nodded and clicked over to her email account. She typed in the address for Layla Michaels, her best friend back on the mainland. Leaving Layla and her other friends behind was one of the only bad parts of moving to the island. It was hard to believe she hadn't talked to Layla in almost two weeks. There was so much to tell her! Abby started to type:

*Hi Layla, it's me!*

*Sorry I haven't written in a while. We've been super busy getting the resort ready to open. And today was our first day with guests. One* of them's a girl our age named Bella Garcia. At dinner tonight, we figured out that we'll be in the same class at school in the fall. Isn't that cool? I already have a new friend and school doesn't start for weeks and weeks! The two of us went kayaking in the mangroves today, which was tons of fun. We saw a bunch of fish and birds, and Bella knew what most of them were. She grew up here in the Florida Keys and knows a lot about all the local wildlife.

Oh! And speaking of cool animals, guess what else I saw today? Dolphins! A bunch of them were swimming right out beyond the lagoon. Rachel says seeing them means good luck. I think she's right!

Abby stopped typing and thought about the dolphins, smiling as she pictured them leaping and playing in the clear blue sea. Then she went back to her email, telling Layla more about the other guests and all the activities that were planned for the week.

After she sent her email, Abby stepped out of the office into the long, whitewashed hallway. The sounds of music and laughter drifted toward her from the huge kitchen at the back of the house. She guessed that the kitchen staff must still be there cleaning up after dinner or preparing for breakfast the next morning.

Abby stuck her head in through the doorway and saw that she was right. The head cook, a local woman named Sofia, was humming along to the radio as she chopped fruit. Several other workers were still there, too, scrubbing pots or adding salt and pepper to the shakers that went on each guest table.

"Abby!" Sofia brushed a strand of curly hair out of her eyes. "Come looking for a bedtime snack, darling?"

Abby smiled. She liked the way Sofia called everyone "darling."

"Actually, I am a little hungry," she said. "I was so busy talking to our guests tonight that I guess I didn't eat enough."

Sofia laughed and patted the seat of a tall stool nearby. "Sit your behind right down and let me make you something," she said. "How about a bowl of arroz con leche?" She winked. "Rice pudding with cinnamon and lemon, just like we make in Cuba."

"Yum!" Abby said eagerly. She already loved all of Sofia's specialties!

Sofia smiled. "My nephew Carlos likes that one, too. He's right around your age." She stepped over to the huge stainless-steel refrigerator. "Maybe you two can meet soon—he lives in Key West, and he was asking about coming to visit the new resort sometime, see where I'm working."

"That would be great," Abby said. "I'd love to meet more kids before school starts."

The rice pudding was delicious. Abby ate it quickly,

listening to Sofia joke around with the staff. She'd just finished the last bite when Sofia glanced out the window. "Look, darling," she told Abby. "There's your cute little friend outside."

"You mean Bella? Maybe I'll go say good night." Abby thanked Sofia for the snack, then hurried outside through the screen door.

Bella and her parents stood by a flowering shrub near the corner of the dining pavilion. They'd stopped to watch a bird fluttering among the leaves. Bella's mother looked over and saw Abby coming.

"Hello, Abby," she said. "We're just taking a short nature walk before bed. Would you like to join us?"

"Sure, thanks!" Abby liked Bella's parents. They both worked at the hospital on Stock Island and were smart and friendly.

The four of them wandered on down the path, watching for wildlife. Soon Bella saw a large, spotted frog.

"That's a leopard frog," she told Abby. "There are lots of them in the Keys."

"He's so cute!" Abby exclaimed, leaning down for a better look. "Maybe I can catch him and keep him as a pet."

For a second, she felt excited about her idea. The apartment complex where she and Daddy had lived back on the mainland hadn't allowed pets.

Then she noticed Bella shaking her head. "You shouldn't do that," she said. "He's a wild animal, and they don't usually make good pets. Frogs need lots of space and water. Plus, you'd have to feed him bugs all the time."

"Bugs? Really?" Abby wrinkled her nose. Before she could say anything else, a loud shriek rang out from the forest nearby. The sound made Mr. Garcia jump.

"Oh my!" he exclaimed. "What on earth was that?"

Bella's mother pointed at a flash of blue and gold

feathers disappearing through the trees. "I think it was a bird," she said. "It looked big!"

"It didn't look or sound like any native bird I've ever seen in the islands around here." Bella sounded surprised. "You don't have a pet parrot, do you, Abby?"

"Nope." Abby shrugged. "There are no pets at all on the island. Yet." She glanced at the frog. "If wild animals don't make good pets, maybe I can talk Daddy into getting me a dog . . ."

Bella was still staring into the trees. "That's weird," she said. "Maybe someone's parrot escaped or something."

"Maybe." Just then Abby heard her father calling her name. She glanced toward the house and saw him on the porch waving at her.

"Layla just emailed back!" he called. "But hurry up if you want to read it tonight—it's almost bedtime."

"Coming!" Abby responded. Then she smiled at Bella and her parents. "Thanks for letting me come on your nature walk. See you at breakfast!"

# 4
# Friends or Not?

The next morning, Abby woke up early. Sunshine poured in through the windows, making the freshly painted yellow walls of her room seem brighter than ever. She quickly pulled on shorts and a T-shirt and headed downstairs.

She was halfway down the steps to the first floor when she heard voices drifting out of the office just below. Daddy and Rachel were in there, and they both sounded worried.

". . . and the Channing family just canceled for the week after next," Rachel was saying. "That means we have only eight guests booked for that week."

"And seven this week, and only six next week." Daddy's voice was solemn. "Do you think we rushed our grand opening? I mean, we haven't even decided what to name the resort yet."

That was true. Abby, Daddy, and Rachel had talked about calling their new business the Barnaby Key Family Resort. That was the name on the website Rachel had set up to advertise the business. But they still weren't sure they liked the name. Daddy thought they should use something catchier—a name that would make people really want to visit.

Rachel's next words chased any thoughts of the name out of Abby's head. "I don't know," she said. "But if we don't get more reservations soon . . ." Her voice trailed off.

Abby gripped the staircase's polished wooden handrail. If they didn't get more reservations, then what? Would the resort have to close? Would they all end up back in that cramped apartment on the mainland, miles from the sea, with no beach or frogs or dolphins anywhere in sight? She couldn't stand the thought.

*We have to book more guests soon!* she thought. *We have to! How could anyone not want to come here?*

Just then Sofia bustled out of the kitchen. She spotted Abby standing on the stairs and waved. "Darling! Can you come help me bring out the fruit bowls? Harvey was supposed to do it, but he's still messing around with the eggs." She shook her head. "That boy . . . ," she muttered, then lapsed into annoyed Spanish.

"Coming," Abby called back, hurrying down the last few steps.

After she set a bowl of fruit on the big breakfast buffet table in the dining pavilion, Abby looked around. The honeymoon couple were sitting by themselves in the far

corner, holding hands over their coffee and toast. Bella's parents were helping themselves to tea, while her aunt and uncle hovered at the far end of the buffet exclaiming over Sofia's homemade pastries. Bella had just finished loading a plate with scrambled eggs and was heading back to her table.

"Hi," Abby greeted her, hurrying over. "Did you sleep okay?"

"Sure." Bella returned her smile. "It's really nice and quiet here." She giggled. "Well, except for the birds. They're louder than my alarm clock at home! They woke me up so early I snuck out and went bird-watching before breakfast."

Abby laughed. "Yeah, it took me a while to get used to hearing their calls first thing in the morning. But I love seeing them flying around everywhere. Did you see anything interesting this morning?"

"Anything interesting?" Bella said, blinking. "Um, what do you mean?"

"Birds, silly! What do you think I mean?" Abby grinned. "You went bird-watching, right?"

"Oh! Right." Bella looked sheepish. "Sure, I saw lots of cool birds." She tilted her head, looking shy. "I could show you after lunch, if you want."

"I'm in!" Abby said eagerly. "Why don't we go before lunch, though? It won't be so hot then."

"Um, I can't," Bella said. "I told my parents I'd do something with them this morning."

"Oh, okay." Abby shrugged. "After lunch is fine. I'd better go help Sofia with the rest of the buffet now. See you after lunch!"

When all the guests had finished their breakfast, Abby and her father helped Sofia and the others clean up. Rachel was busy helping the maid tidy the bungalows. That was one thing Abby had already learned about running a resort. Everyone pitched in!

While her father scrubbed the egg pans, Abby wondered if she should ask him about what she'd overheard earlier. Was the resort already in trouble? But she decided to stay quiet—at least for now. She was sure that more and more people would want to come to Barnaby Key once they heard how nice the resort was.

Soon the breakfast dishes were clean. Sofia and her helpers started chopping vegetables for lunch.

"Can I help?" Abby offered, picking up a cucumber.

Sofia waved her hand in a shooing motion. "Run along and have some fun, darling," she said. "We've got it covered in here."

Abby's father nodded. "If you want to help, you could check on the guests," he told Abby. "Make sure they don't need anything."

"Okay, I can do that." Abby said good-bye to her father and the kitchen staff. Then she headed outside. She could hear voices from the direction of the beach, so she walked that way.

The honeymooners were taking photos of each other in the surf, giggling and striking funny poses. Watching from some beach chairs nearby were Bella's parents, aunt, and uncle. But Bella was nowhere in sight.

*That's weird*, Abby thought. *Bella said she promised to hang out with her family this morning.*

She was about to go over and ask after her new friend. But then she noticed Rachel struggling to pull a loaded laundry cart over the shell path nearby. "Hold on!" Abby called. "I'll help you."

She stayed busy all morning, first helping Rachel and then showing the honeymooners how to use the kayaks. Abby didn't think about Bella again until she saw her stepping into the dining pavilion for lunch.

"Hey," she said then, hurrying over. "There you are! I looked for you on the beach this morning."

"Oh." Bella bit her lip and looked away. "Um, I had a stomachache. I think I ate too much for breakfast. So I went to lie down for a while."

"Oh no!" Abby felt concerned. "Are you okay? Should I ask my dad to call a doctor?"

"No, no, I'm fine!" Bella said quickly. "I feel great now."

"Good." Abby was still a little worried. Bella must have felt really sick to stay in the cabin all morning! "Do you want to do our bird-watching walk another day?"

"No," Bella said with a little frown.

Abby was surprised. Did Bella mean she didn't want to change their plans to a different day—or that she didn't want to hang out with Abby at all?

Before she could ask, though, Bella laughed. "I mean, yes, let's go bird-watching another time," she said. "But not because I feel sick or anything. It's so hot, though—why don't we go snorkeling in the lagoon instead?"

Abby was relieved. "That sounds great—let's go!"

The two of them had a great time snorkeling. Even though Bella was shy, once she started talking, Abby realized how smart and funny she was. Abby was glad that she and Bella would be going to the same school in Key West in the fall so they could still spend time together even after the Garcias left the resort.

After dinner that night, Abby's father announced that there would be a campfire and sing-along on the beach. "Everyone's invited," he said. "Meet us there in half an hour!"

Abby helped her family and the staff clean up, as usual. When they arrived at the beach, the guests were already there waiting.

Well, most of them were, anyway. "Where's Bella?" Abby asked Mr. and Mrs. Garcia.

"She'll be along soon," Bella's dad said. "She's changing her sandals, I think."

But fifteen minutes later, Bella still hadn't shown up. Feeling a little worried, Abby decided to check on her. She headed to the Silver Palm Bungalow, but it was empty.

"That's weird," Abby whispered, standing on the

cabin's little front porch and wondering what to do. Where could Bella be?

She returned to the beach. Daddy had the bonfire going, and Rachel was leading the group in a funny song.

Abby tapped Mr. Garcia on the arm. "I just checked, and Bella isn't in your bungalow," she said.

"Really?" He looked a little surprised.

But Mrs. Garcia just laughed. "I imagine she saw a pretty bird and took off after it to try to get a photo," she told Abby.

Abby nodded. Bella's parents knew her better than anyone. If they weren't worried, Abby guessed she shouldn't be, either.

Still, she couldn't help watching for the other girl to arrive. Finally, just as it was getting dark, Bella stepped onto the beach. She was wearing sneakers and carrying a camera.

Abby hurried over. "You're finally here!" she exclaimed. "Where were you?"

Bella looked startled. "Nowhere," she said. "I mean, in the bungalow getting my camera."

"But I came by," Abby said. "You weren't there."

Bella frowned. "Why were you checking on me? I was fine." She pushed past Abby. "Excuse me, I want to sit with my family."

Abby watched her hurry away, feeling confused and a little hurt. She hadn't meant to make Bella mad, but she'd kind of sounded that way just now. Did she want to be Abby's friend or not?

# 5

## Early Morning Mystery

That night, Abby dreamed about being a dolphin. She swam around, breathed through a blowhole, and did jumps and leaps through the waves. It was fun!

Then Dolphin-Abby saw Bella snorkeling nearby. She waved a fin at her, but instead of waving back, Bella opened her mouth and let out a loud, terrified cry! Dolphin-Abby tried to tell her she just wanted to be friends, but Bella kept on squawking and squawking . . .

Abby suddenly woke up and sat up in bed. It had

been a dream! But then the screech came again—from right outside her window!

She got up and looked outside. Dawn was just breaking over the eastern horizon, and all sorts of birds were chirping and singing. Then a couple of small birds suddenly darted past and dove into the bushes at the back of the cleared yard. Abby gasped as a larger bird flew up and let out another squawk.

"A parrot!" she whispered. The bird had a blue back, a yellow front, and a long tail. It let out one last loud cry and then flew off into the woods with the smaller birds diving after it.

Abby yanked on some clothes and rushed downstairs, hoping for another glimpse of the colorful bird. Was it the same one she'd spotted on the nature walk with Bella's family? And why were the smaller birds chasing it?

She stopped on the porch, glancing around for movement. Instead of the bird, she saw Bella tiptoeing across the grass toward an untamed section of forest beyond the volleyball court. A second later, Bella disappeared into the thick underbrush.

Abby blinked, wondering if she was still dreaming. It was very early. Sofia hadn't even started breakfast yet. Why was Bella wandering off into the woods all by herself?

Feeling curious, Abby kicked on a pair of Rachel's sandals that were by the door. They were a little too big, but she hardly noticed. She couldn't help thinking back on the times Bella had disappeared. First after breakfast yesterday, then again after dinner. Was she about to find out where Bella had gone—and why?

For a second, Abby felt guilty. She didn't like the thought of spying on her new friend. But what if Bella was in trouble? There was no good reason for her to sneak away into the wild forest. At least not one that Abby could think of.

She hurried across the grass. It was easy to figure out which way Bella had gone—there were a couple of broken branches and footprints in the soft ground at the edge of the woods. Once she pushed through the first tangle of vines and brush, Abby found herself on a narrow but well-worn dirt trail.

*Bella didn't make this herself,* she thought. *It must be an animal trail. I wonder if there are Key deer here after all.*

Abby kept an eye out for paw or hoof prints. But the sun wasn't all the way up yet and the light was dim. She did spot a few more human footprints, though.

The trail wound around some big trees and a couple of rocky spots. Soon Abby lost track of which direction she was going. Luckily, there were no forks in the trail, so she knew it would be easy to find her way back.

*Back from where?* she wondered, once again feeling curious. *Where is Bella going?*

She got the answer to that question just a few minutes later. The trail suddenly ended in a large clearing—at the rocky shore of a cove Abby had never seen before!

"Whoa!" she exclaimed aloud, so surprised that she forgot to be quiet.

Bella stood at the edge of the water. She spun around at Abby's voice.

"Hey," Bella said. "What are you doing here?"

Abby stepped out of the shady forest into the clearing. "I was about to ask you that," she said.

Bella scowled. "Did you follow me? That's not very nice."

"Sorry," Abby said. "But what difference does it make? This place is cool!"

She looked around. How had she and her parents missed this cove? She guessed it opened into the sea on the far side of the island, opposite the beach and lagoon. They didn't take the boats that way very often, since the water was a little rougher over there. But the cove itself was quiet and sheltered, with only a narrow channel leading out and lots of big rocks and trees protecting it from the wind and waves.

Bella took a step toward her, still looking unhappy. "You should go back," she said.

"Why?" Abby blinked at her, a little annoyed by how secretive the other girl was acting. "Look, if you don't want to be my friend, that's fine. But this is my family's island, and I can go anywhere I—"

She cut herself off with a gasp. Because several gray snouts had just poked up out of the water a few yards from shore.

"Whoa," Abby exclaimed. "Dolphins!"

# 6

## Bella's Secret

The dolphins quickly disappeared, but a moment later, one leaped all the way out of the water, her skin gleaming gray under the rising sun. Then another dolphin jumped into view, and another . . .

For a second, Abby couldn't move or speak. She couldn't seem to stop staring at the playful dolphins leaping and chasing one another around the cove. "They're so beautiful," she blurted out at last. "Did you see them?"

Bella's shoulders slumped. "Yeah, I know," she said. "That's why I've been coming here. I followed a big parrot this way yesterday morning before breakfast and found this cove. That's when I first spotted them. It's a pod of bottlenose dolphins. I think they come here a lot." She shrugged. "At least, they were here when I snuck back after breakfast, and again before the bonfire."

Abby's eyes widened. So that was why Bella kept disappearing!

"You mean *during* the bonfire," she corrected Bella with a smile. "You missed most of the sing-along, you know."

Bella frowned again for a second, then laughed. "Sorry about the way I acted last night," she said. "I wanted to tell you about the dolphins, especially since I know you like them, too." She glanced out at the frolicking animals. "But I sort of wanted to keep it a secret, too, you know?"

Abby didn't really know why she would want to keep something like that a secret. But she was glad that Bella was acting friendly again, so she just nodded.

Then she turned to watch the dolphins. "How many are there? Can you tell?"

"I've spotted at least five, maybe six," Bella said. "There—that one, the big one that just jumped? I call him Rascal. He's super playful."

Abby laughed. "I like it!" she said. "What about the rest? Do they have names, too?"

"The smaller, more slender one over there is Graygirl." She shrugged. "That's all I've come up with so far."

"Those are good names." Abby stepped closer, watching for another dolphin to appear. She smiled when one poked his head up and let out a sharp cry. "That's a talkative one," she said. "Let's call him Echo."

She and Bella watched the dolphins for a few more minutes. At first it was hard to keep track of which one was which. But before long Abby saw that they were all a little different. There was a big, stout dolphin they decided to call Neptune. And a bossy one they named Nana, after Bella's bossy grandmother.

"What about that one?" Bella pointed as another dolphin appeared above the water. "He has a few little spots on his back, see?"

"Yeah." Abby thought for a second. "What about Domino?"

"Perfect!" Bella giggled. "You're really good at thinking of names."

"Thanks." Abby watched as Domino dove out of sight beneath the surface. "I can't believe all these dolphins were right here all along, and I didn't even know it. I'm glad you found them."

"Well, I'm glad my family decided to come here," Bella said. "I've never seen dolphins so close-up before. It's amazing."

Abby smiled at her. "Yeah." Just then Rascal poked his head out of the water, seeming to grin at the girls. "Look," she said. "Rascal says to come on in, the water's fine."

Bella laughed. "Sure—if you're a dolphin!"

"No, really." Abby took a step closer. "The water's

really calm in this cove. Let's try going in. Maybe the dolphins will let us swim with them!"

"Are you serious?" Bella sounded nervous. "We can't do that. They're wild animals! Besides, our parents wouldn't want us to swim with no adults nearby."

Abby bit her lip. Bella was right—the rule on the island was that kids couldn't swim unless there was an adult within eyesight.

"Okay," she said. "But look, the water's really shallow at the edge. We could just wade in a little bit."

"I don't know . . ." Bella still sounded nervous, but she was watching the dolphins with a longing look in her eyes.

"Come on, it'll be fine." Abby kicked off Rachel's shoes, then fished her phone out of her pocket and set it carefully on one of them. After that, she stepped into the water. The rocks poked her feet, but she didn't mind. "We won't go in very far—promise," she said.

Bella hesitated. But when Abby took another step,

Bella slipped off her own shoes and followed her in. "I hope we don't scare them away," Bella said, watching the dolphins.

"We won't." Abby took another step. The water had almost reached her waist now. "Look! Rascal just swam closer."

Bella gasped. "You're right! I guess he really is the bravest, just like I thought."

Abby held out her hand. "Here, Rascal!" she crooned. "It's okay, we won't hurt you."

The dolphin stayed where he was for a moment, watching them with his wide, curious dark eyes. Nana and Echo surfaced right behind him. Nana let out an anxious squeak, but Echo crowded up right behind Rascal.

"It's okay, you guys," Bella said softly. "We're your friends."

Rascal chirped uncertainly. Abby held her breath as he drifted forward a little more. Closer, closer . . .

Then, with a sudden burst of movement, he zipped right past the girls! Abby reached out and felt his slick, rubbery skin, which somehow seemed warm and cool at the same time, sliding under her fingers.

"Oh!" she cried. "I touched him!"

The dolphins were all back out in deeper water by now. Rascal and a couple of the others surfaced again, watching the girls.

But Abby hardly saw them. She stared at her hand in amazement. She'd just touched a real live dolphin. This had to be one of the best moments of her entire life!

# 7

# Cross My Heart

Abby and Bella spent another hour with the dolphins, watching them play and occasionally reaching out to touch them as they swam by. The longer they stayed, the less nervous Rascal and Echo seemed about coming close, though the rest of the pod still kept their distance.

Then, as if on cue, all the dolphins turned and swam off toward the mouth of the cove. Soon they'd disappeared from sight. The girls waited a few minutes, but the pod seemed to have left for the deeper waters of the ocean.

"They probably went to find something to eat," Abby guessed. "Maybe they'll be back later."

Bella glanced up at the sky. It was brighter and warmer in the clearing than when they'd first arrived. "How long have we been here?"

"I'm not sure." Abby waded back to dry ground to check her phone. As soon as she picked it up, she realized something. "Oh! I should have taken pictures." Then she gulped as she saw the time on the screen. "Oops. We've been gone a while. I hope nobody missed us and started to worry."

"Me too," Bella said.

"I'll text my dad and tell him we're okay." Abby quickly opened a text message:

*Hi! Bella and I went for a walk. Be back soon to help with breakfast.*

He texted back almost right away:

*Glad u texted! Leave a note next time ok? We figured u two were together but were starting to worry.*

Abby felt guilty. "I guess they did miss us," she told Bella. "I'll explain about the dolphins—then he'll understand why we lost track of time."

"No!" Bella grabbed Abby's arm before she could hit another letter on her phone. "Don't tell him about the dolphins, okay?"

"What?" Abby blinked at her in surprise. "Why not?"

Bella shrugged. "I just thought it could be, you know, our secret."

Abby didn't understand. "A secret?" she echoed. "But why? I want to share the beautiful dolphins with my family—with everyone!"

Bella bit her lip, looking anxious. "I don't know if

that's a good idea," she said. "I mean, if too many people visit the cove, the dolphins might stop coming here so much. And your parents would probably want to clear a bigger path, and then even more people would come . . ."

Abby frowned, still not quite getting it. "But the dolphins are so friendly! They probably wouldn't mind."

"What if they do, though? Should we take that chance?" Bella glanced out toward the still water of the cove. "I'm pretty sure I can convince my parents to come back here to Barnaby Key a lot. We have tons of family visiting from up north, and I'm sure they'd all love the resort. The two of us can still come to the cove together whenever I'm here. It'll be our special secret."

Abby still didn't understand why Bella was so anxious to keep the dolphins a secret. But she did like the thought of her family coming to the resort a lot. Maybe

that would help Daddy and Rachel feel less worried about the business.

Besides, she didn't want to upset her new friend. "Okay, I guess," she said. "It's our secret. But we'd better go back now."

The two girls parted ways once they reached the edge of the woods. It was so warm that their shorts were already dry, but Bella said she wanted to change her shoes before breakfast. With a quick wave, she hurried across the lawn toward her bungalow. Abby watched her go, thinking over everything that had just happened.

Suddenly, there was a flash of bright blue in the trees off to her right. Abby spun around, trying to see if it was the big parrot she'd spotted earlier. But whatever it was had already disappeared.

"Oh well," Abby said aloud, startling a lizard that had been drowsing on a branch nearby. "I guess I'd better get inside and help with breakfast. Maybe Bella can help me look for that bird later—when we go back to see the dolphins."

She smiled and shivered, still hardly believing what she'd just seen in the secret cove. Then she headed toward the house.

# 8

## Carlos

The kitchen was bustling with breakfast preparations. Rachel headed out toward the pavilion with a pot of coffee, while Sofia stirred a big pan of eggs on the stove. Abby's dad and the other kitchen employees were busy, too.

Then Abby noticed someone new. A boy around her age perched on a stool next to the stove. He had dark hair and wide-set brown eyes.

Just then Sofia looked up and spotted Abby. "Darling!"

she called. "Come meet Carlos. I told you about him the other day."

Abby hurried over. Carlos slid down from the stool and stared at her curiously. "Hi," he said. "How old are you? Tía Sofia wasn't sure."

"I just turned eight," she said. "I'm Abby."

"Yeah, I know." Carlos shrugged and stuck his hands in the pockets of his shorts. "Your family just moved here from the mainland."

"That's right. I guess Sofia told you that, huh?" Abby glanced at the cook, but Sofia had returned to her work. "And you live in Key West, right?"

"Uh-huh. I'm a conch—that means born and raised in the Keys." Carlos stood up a little straighter, looking proud. "My parents run a tourist fishing business. It's super successful."

"That's nice." He seemed a little stuck-up, but Abby didn't say so. "I hope our resort will be successful, too."

"Maybe it will." Carlos sounded dubious. He stepped over and grabbed a muffin off a platter on the counter, stuffing it into his mouth. "I mean, people will probably come from all around for Tía Sofia's cooking," he mumbled while chewing the muffin. "At least you've got her and a few other conchs to help, since y'all aren't from around here."

Abby frowned, wondering if that was supposed to be an insult. But Carlos was smiling, so she shrugged it off.

"Hey, since you're from the Keys, I have a question," she said. "I saw this huge blue bird flying into the woods—like a big parrot, you know? Some smaller birds were chasing it."

"A big blue parrot?" Carlos looked surprised. Then he nodded. "Oh, wait—maybe it's Bogart!"

"What's a Bogart?" Abby asked, ducking aside as one of the waiters rushed past with a pitcher of freshly squeezed orange juice.

"Not what—who," Carlos said. "This tourist named

Mr. Robinson came down to fish with us for a whole month earlier this summer. He's from, like, Atlanta or somewhere, I think? Anyway, he brought his pet macaw with him—that's Bogart."

"And the macaw escaped?" Abby said. "That's terrible!"

Carlos shook his head. "Bogart didn't escape," he said. "Mr. Robinson decided he was too much trouble to take care of, so he let him go wild."

Abby gasped. "But that's so mean!"

"Yeah, Mr. Robinson was kind of a jerk," Carlos agreed, licking the last crumbs of the muffin from his fingers. "He was rude to everyone, and he never left a tip. Anyway, one day he rented a boat and said he was taking Bogart out to see some of the smaller islands. I guess that's when he let him go. By the time anyone heard about it, the bird was gone." He glanced at Sofia, who was too far away to hear their conversation. "Tía Sofia and some of her friends went out searching a couple of times, but they weren't even sure which way Mr. Robinson had gone. So we all figured Bogart was . . ." He drew his finger across his throat. Abby knew what that meant: They'd thought the macaw was dead.

"Wow," she said. "I guess he survived after all."

"Are you sure you really saw a bird like that?" Carlos seemed interested. "It wasn't just a heron or something?"

"No!" Abby felt a little insulted. "I might be new to the islands, but I'm a lifelong Florida girl. I know what a heron looks like. This bird was brighter blue, with yellow on his belly."

Carlos nodded. "Okay. Maybe we should go look for him."

Just then Abby's father rushed past. "Hurry up, kids," he sang out. "The food's going fast this morning— guess all the fresh sea air is making our guests hungry! You'd better get out there if you don't want to miss out."

"Coming," Abby called after him. She glanced at

Carlos. "Right after breakfast I can show you where I saw the bird, okay?"

Half an hour later, the two of them were in the woods. Abby stopped on the deer path, glancing around.

"The last time I saw him, he was over there." She pointed in the direction where she'd seen the flash of blue.

"Okay." Carlos leaned down to examine the trail. "Hey, I bet you have Key deer here. Let's follow the trail and see if we can spot any. They're really rare, you know."

"I know," Abby said quickly. "But like I said, Bogart flew that way."

Carlos took a few steps along the trail. "We can look for him later."

"No!" Abby gulped, remembering her promise to Bella. She couldn't let Carlos follow the trail, or he'd find the secret cove! "Look, if you don't want to search

64

for Bogart, I should go back and help clean up the breakfast stuff."

Carlos snorted. "Whatever," he said. "If you're afraid of running into an iguana out here, just say so!"

"I'm not afraid," Abby snapped. "I just didn't come out here to look for deer right now."

"Sure, if you say so." Carlos smirked. "Call me if you see that bird again, okay? Or a heron."

For a second, Abby thought he was going to keep walking along the trail. Instead, he turned and headed out of the woods. With a silent sigh of relief, she followed.

# 9

## Dolphin Magic

Right after lunch, Abby and Bella waited until nobody was looking, then ducked into the woods. This time they brought along life jackets and kickboards. That was Bella's idea.

"I still don't think we should go out very far," she warned as the two of them hurried along the trail toward the cove. "But maybe we can float out a tiny bit closer to the pod."

"Sounds good," Abby said. "Look, we're almost to Dolphin Cove."

"Dolphin Cove?" Bella smiled. "That's what I was calling it in my head, too."

Abby giggled. "When something like that happens, Daddy always says, 'Great minds think alike!'"

The dolphins were playing in the water when the girls emerged into the clearing. "Look, there's Domino!" Bella cried as the spotted dolphin did a graceful leap.

Abby was already pulling on her life jacket. "Let's go in," she said. She raced toward the water's edge, then stopped. "Oh, wait—first I want to take some video."

She pulled out her phone and switched to the camera app. The dolphins looked pretty small through the viewfinder, so she carefully stepped onto a line of rocks jutting out into the deeper water. Then she started filming the dolphins. Right away, Rascal did a dramatic spinning jump. He landed with a huge splash, almost bumping into Neptune. Water splashed up over the rocky spit, getting Abby's legs wet.

"I think he's showing off for the camera," she said with a laugh. "Come on, let's go in."

Soon the two girls were floating on their kickboards. The dolphins didn't move away at all. "I think they recognize us," Abby said as she watched Graygirl glide past just beneath the surface.

"I think so, too," Bella said. "Look—Echo is almost close enough to touch!" She stretched out her hand. But the dolphin dodged away at the last second.

"Aw, don't be shy," Abby called to him.

Bella laughed. "It's okay," she said. "I'm happy just being close to them."

At that moment, Rascal's head popped out of the water. He let out a chirpy little whistle.

"I wonder what he's saying." Abby moved her legs underwater to turn and face the playful dolphin. "Sorry, Rascal. We don't speak Dolphin."

"We could try." Bella took a breath, then let out a whistle.

Domino surfaced, staring at her curiously. Then Rascal whistled again.

"Hey, I think you're talking to them!" Abby exclaimed. "Let me try . . ."

For the next few minutes, they experimented with making different whistles and chirps. Sometimes the dolphins ignored them. Other times they seemed to listen and respond. Eventually they settled on a certain whistle that made Rascal and Domino swim closer almost every time.

"I'm still not sure what we're saying to them," Abby said with a laugh. "But I think they like it!"

After almost two hours, the girls reluctantly decided to go back. "We shouldn't stay out here for very long at a time," Bella said as she led the way onto the rocky shore. "Otherwise our parents might start to wonder what we're doing."

Abby picked up her phone and slipped on her flip-flops. "Are you sure we shouldn't just tell them?" she said, glancing out at the dolphins. "I'm sure the dolphins wouldn't leave if more people started coming. They're super friendly."

"No! You promised," Bella said quickly. "It's our secret, remember?"

"I remember." Abby swallowed back a sigh. She still didn't understand why Bella didn't want to share the dolphins with everyone.

When they were back at the resort, Bella went to change out of her swimsuit. Abby wandered off to find her parents. They weren't in the office or on the beach with the rest of the guests. She decided to check upstairs. When she was almost to the third floor, she heard voices coming from her parents' bedroom.

". . . and I was thinking maybe adding more activities would help us compete with the other resorts," Rachel was saying. "Sofia suggested cooking classes."

Abby froze where she was. Oh no! Were her parents still worrying about going out of business?

"That's a good idea," Daddy told Rachel. "I could build some trails to attract mountain bikers. And maybe plant more flowers?"

"That would be nice." Rachel sighed. "I don't know if it's enough, though. We need something special—something to make us stand out."

"Okay, but what?" Daddy said.

Suddenly, Abby knew the answer. She raced up the last few steps. "I know what would make everyone want to come here!" she cried. "Dolphin Cove!"

# 10

## Telling the Truth

At first Daddy and Rachel were confused. But when Abby explained about Dolphin Cove, they got excited.

"A pod of dolphins, right here on our island?" Rachel exclaimed.

"Can you take us there?" Daddy added.

"Sure." Abby was thrilled to see them so happy. "It's only a short walk through the forest. We can go right now if you want."

"Great," Daddy said.

Rachel checked her watch. "Wait—not great," she said. "It's almost dinnertime, and then we've scheduled a movie on the beach afterward, remember? We'll have to check out the dolphins in the morning. Okay, Abs?"

"Okay," Abby agreed.

But this time her smile felt forced. She'd just realized something—she'd spilled the secret! What would Bella say when she found out?

*I have to tell her right away*, Abby thought. *It's only fair.*

But in the rush to get ready for dinner, she didn't have a moment alone with Bella until after the meal had ended. Then she managed to drag her off behind the pavilion.

"What is it?" Bella was staring over toward the beach, where some of the resort employees were setting up a big movie screen. "I don't want to miss the start of the movie."

"I know. But this is important." Abby took a deep breath. "I, um, sort of told my parents about Dolphin Cove."

"What?" Bella spun to face her. "You're joking, right?"

"No. I'm sorry." Abby started to tell her about the conversation she'd overheard. But she'd only managed a few words before Bella cut her off.

"You promised!" she cried, her brown eyes flashing with fury. "I can't believe it—I thought we were friends!"

"We are!" Abby exclaimed. "Bella, wait, just let me explain . . ."

But Bella was already stomping off toward the beach. Abby's shoulders slumped. Had she ruined their friendship for good this time?

Abby barely paid attention to the movie. She sat on the warm sand beside Rachel, trying not to stare at Bella, who was sitting between her mother and her uncle.

*Maybe I shouldn't have told*, Abby thought. *Maybe I should have kept my promise to Bella and kept the cove a secret.*

Then she shook her head. That was silly. Her parents

would have found the cove eventually. And by telling them now, maybe she could help the resort attract more guests.

*Still, maybe I could have waited* a little *longer to tell them*, she thought with a sigh, sneaking another peek at Bella. *I probably could have convinced Bella to let me tell eventually. And that way we'd still be friends . . .*

She was still worrying about what had happened when the movie ended. Most of the guests headed to the dining pavilion for a late-night snack. But Abby wasn't hungry. She stayed on the beach to help Daddy dismantle the movie projector.

"Thanks, Abby," he said. "I'll take the equipment back to the house. Why don't you go see if Rachel needs any help in the dining room."

"Okay." Abby felt nervous about seeing Bella. But when she entered the dining pavilion, Bella was nowhere in sight.

Rachel spotted Abby and rushed over. "We're out of mint for the iced tea," she said. "Would you mind picking some? There's a patch in the herb garden."

"Sure." Abby headed outside again. The herb garden was behind the house near the volleyball and croquet courts.

She walked slowly in that direction. The sun had set, but there was still plenty of moonlight to see by. A cool breeze tickled Abby's face. It felt good after the heat of the summer day.

Daddy had taught Abby all about herbs and other plants over the years. She spotted the mint immediately. Before she could bend down to pick it, though, she saw a flash of bright blue out of the corner of her eye.

She spun around. "Bogart?" she whispered, squinting into the forest.

There! Between the trees, she'd seen another flash of blue and gold. It was the missing macaw—it had to be!

Abby rushed forward, pushing her way into the moonlit forest. Which way had Bogart gone?

Suddenly, a loud squawk rang out from deeper in the trees. The bird sounded scared!

"It's okay, Bogart!" Abby called. "I'm coming!"

She raced down the deer trail. There were a couple more terrified shrieks from the bird, though she still couldn't see him.

Before she knew it, she burst out into a clearing. It was Dolphin Cove! Abby had been so distracted that she hadn't really noticed which way she was heading.

But now she saw where she was—and that she wasn't alone. Bella stood at the edge of the water. She wasn't looking at the dolphins, though they were bobbing in the waves just offshore. Instead, she was staring into the underbrush.

"Oh!" Abby blurted out, suddenly nervous about facing her friend—or ex-friend?

Bella spun around. But she didn't look mad—just anxious.

"I just saw a raccoon chasing after a big blue parrot," she told Abby, pointing into the woods a few yards from where she was standing. "I think the bird might be injured. We have to help it!"

# 11

## Rescue Mission

Abby forgot all about her fight with Bella. "That's Bogart!" she cried. "I thought he sounded scared—now I know why. That raccoon wants to eat him for dinner!"

"Come on." Bella was already hurrying toward the woods. "Grab a stick or something. Maybe we can scare off the raccoon. But be careful—they can be mean!"

"Okay." Abby grabbed the thickest stick she could find. Then she followed her friend into the woods.

It was much darker under the trees. Spooky shadows seemed to dart around the girls' feet, though Abby told herself they were probably made by cute little lizards or frogs.

"Bogart!" she called. "Are you in here?"

A loud squawk rang out from just ahead. "This way!" Bella said. "There they are!"

Abby spotted them, too. Bogart was flapping along the ground, dragging one wing. "You're right—he definitely looks injured!" she exclaimed. "Hey, you mean bully," she called out to the raccoon. "Leave him alone!"

The raccoon stopped and spun around. That gave the macaw a chance to flap away out of sight. The raccoon chattered angrily at the girls, then darted off in the same direction.

"Oh no," Bella said. "He's still after the parrot! I think they went this way . . ."

Abby followed close behind her. Just ahead they both could hear the animals crashing through the underbrush.

"Now they're turning that way, I think." Abby pointed off to the right.

Bella nodded and changed directions. There was a big clump of thorny vines in the way, and it took them a few moments to carefully step around them. By that time, the sounds were fading a little. But then another squawk rang out.

Abby tilted her head, trying to figure out where it was coming from. Somehow, noises sounded different in the dark. "I think they're heading toward the cove again," she said.

"I think you're right." Bella was already changing directions. "Let's go!"

Soon the girls burst back into the clearing. Abby gasped. The raccoon was there—and he was creeping toward Bogart! The macaw edged toward the water, still dragging his injured wing.

"Quit that!" Bella cried.

"Let's go!" Abby brandished her stick and stepped forward. But Bella stopped her.

"Don't get too close," she warned. "If that raccoon hasn't run away by now, he's not scared of us. He might bite if we go over there."

Abby knew Bella was right. But they couldn't let him grab the poor macaw!

Bogart crept just out of reach. But he was running out of space. He hopped up onto the first of the line of rocks that jutted out into the water. The raccoon followed.

"Uh-oh," Bella said. "Now he's trapped on that little spit!"

She was right. The raccoon blocked the only path back to dry land. "Too bad Bogart can't swim like the dolphins," Abby said. Then her eyes widened as she got an idea.

She pursed her lips—and let out a loud whistle! The raccoon jumped and spun around again.

"That won't stop him for long," Bella said. Sure enough, the raccoon soon crawled out across one of the rocks, then another.

"I know." Abby was watching the water. She smiled when Rascal's head popped up. She whistled again, and the dolphin zoomed closer—sending a wave of water over the rocky spit!

Bella gasped as Bogart was washed into the cove. "Oh no!" she cried.

"Oh yes." Abby kicked off her shoes. Out of the corner of her eye, she saw the raccoon dashing off into the forest, looking wet and disgruntled. "Now we can rescue Bogart!"

She rushed into the shallows. But Bella grabbed her arm.

"You can't go in there!" she cried. "It's nighttime, and you don't have a life jacket or anything! Anyway, I can't see the bird anywhere."

Abby couldn't see Bogart, either. But the dolphins

were gathering in one spot near the end of the spit, their gray heads bobbing in the dim light.

She fished her phone out of her pocket. "Here," she said, turning it on and handing it to Bella. "If anything happens, use this to call someone."

Without waiting for a response, she plunged into the dark water.

Swimming in the dark was scary, especially when Abby felt something brush past her leg. But she relaxed when a slender gray shape appeared beside her. It was Graygirl.

"Help me find Bogart, okay?" Abby whispered.

The dolphin swam closer, nudging her a little to the left. Abby went the way the dolphin was pushing her. A second later, she saw Rascal's head pop up. He let out a whistle, then disappeared underwater again.

Now Abby saw the rest of the pod just ahead. She swam toward them. When she got closer, she saw Nana nosing at something—a limp blue form in the water.

It was Bogart! A second later, Neptune swam in and nosed at the bird, too. Bogart let out a weak squawk and flapped one waterlogged wing. Next, Domino nudged at him, turning him slightly so his head stayed above water.

Suddenly, Abby understood what was happening. *They're helping him!* she thought in awe. *The dolphins are working together to keep Bogart from sinking!*

# 12

## New Name, New Friends

Abby pushed gently past Domino. "Excuse me, guys," she said as she treaded water. "I've got him, okay?"

She reached out carefully. The macaw squawked and flopped when she touched him. But she was able to grab him around the breast, which felt surprisingly slender and light beneath the wet feathers. Finally, Bogart relaxed.

"Thank you," he squawked.

Abby was so surprised she almost dropped him. "You talk!" she exclaimed.

She half expected him to reply, "Why, yes, of course I do, you silly girl!"

Instead, he let out a soft coo, then said, "Thank you, thank you, you're welcome!"

Abby smiled, suddenly remembering that some parrots could be trained to say a few words. "Yes, you are—very welcome," she said. "Now let's get you back to shore so you can dry off. Coming, guys?"

She glanced at the dolphins surrounding her, all of them bobbing quietly in the dark water. When she started swimming carefully back to shore with one arm, Bogart clutched in the other, she wasn't alone. The entire pod flanked her until the water got too shallow for them to go any farther.

A little over an hour later, Abby's hair was almost dry and everyone at the resort had calmed down a little. As soon as Abby had plunged into the water, Bella had called Abby's parents because she was too scared to wait. Daddy and Rachel had arrived moments after Abby emerged with Bogart. Right behind them were Sofia, one of the maids, and most of the other guests.

As soon as Sofia got a look at the bird, she'd confirmed that it was, indeed, Bogart, the missing blue-and-gold macaw that Carlos had mentioned. Then she'd called a friend from Key West who was a vet. He'd promised to come out by boat immediately to take a look at the bird's wing and make sure his time in the water hadn't harmed him.

While they waited in the dining pavilion for the vet to arrive, Abby's parents reminded her that swimming without an adult was dangerous. That was why it was a rule. But they agreed not to punish her for breaking it—*this* time.

"But only because it was for a good cause," Rachel said, giving Bogart a pat.

Abby's father nodded. "Next time, though . . ."

"Don't worry, Daddy," Abby said quickly. "There won't be a next time. I promise."

After that, Sofia told the entire group the same story Carlos had told Abby. And since his previous owner didn't want him back, Abby's parents agreed that Bogart would make an outstanding mascot for their resort.

"You'll have to help me build him a shelter," Abby's father had warned her. "It'll be quite a project. And you'll have to learn how to take care of him properly. You can ask the vet about the basics, then do more research online."

"I will," Abby said, stroking Bogart on his sleek blue head. The macaw perched on the table in front of her. His wing still hung awkwardly, but he looked much calmer now that a mean raccoon wasn't stalking him. He even managed to peck at some berries Sofia had brought him from the kitchen. "I can't believe I finally have a pet!" Abby said as she watched him.

Rachel chuckled. "You certainly found a dramatic way to get him," she joked. "You're a lucky bird, Bogart."

"I'm a pretty bird," Bogart replied in his hoarse, funny voice.

Everyone laughed. "You certainly are," Bella's aunt said.

Mrs. Smith-Patel glanced around at the resort, which looked peaceful beneath the milky light of the moon. "This has certainly been a honeymoon to remember," she said. "Maybe we should come back for our first anniversary."

Her husband nodded. "Sounds like a plan."

"We'll be glad to have you back anytime," Daddy said. "Everyone is welcome here at Dolphin Island Family Resort." He winked at Abby.

She smiled. Her father had finally done it—he'd come up with the perfect name for the business! And once everyone heard about the friendly dolphin pod, Abby was sure people would come from far and wide to visit!

Daddy turned to Rachel and said something about clearing a more direct path to the cove right away. Rachel wanted to put in some benches where people could sit to watch the dolphins.

"But we'll want to keep it as natural as possible," she added. "It's such a lovely place as it is."

Abby nodded her agreement. She loved hearing their plans, but she was a little distracted. Bella hadn't said much since they got back to the resort. Right now she sat across the table from Abby, watching Bogart eat.

Abby stood up and walked over to her. "Can I talk to you for a sec?"

"Sure." Bella followed her to the edge of the pavilion, out of earshot of the adults.

Then she sat down on the steps facing the beach. Abby sat beside her.

"So are you still mad at me?" she blurted out. "About telling the secret, I mean."

Bella looked down at her feet. Then she shot Abby a sidelong look. "I guess not," she said. "Maybe you were right about sharing the dolphins. I was just worried that bringing lots of people to the cove would change things too much."

"Sometimes change is good." Abby shrugged. "Anyway, I only told Daddy and Rachel because I thought it would help the resort. And I was worried."

Bella looked surprised. "Worried about what?"

Abby told her what she'd overheard her parents saying about needing more guests. ". . . so I thought the dolphins would make more people want to come here," she finished.

"They definitely will," Bella said with a nod. She bit her lip. "I just hope . . ."

Abby guessed what she was thinking. "Don't worry, my parents will be careful not to hurt the dolphins. Rachel even said they want to keep the cove as natural as they can."

"I know." Bella glanced over her shoulder toward the others. "They're really cool. I'm sorry I acted like a jerk."

"You didn't!" Abby assured her. "And I'm really sorry, too. I should have talked to you before I told them about the cove." She shrugged. "Sometimes my mouth gets ahead of my brain—at least that's what Daddy says."

Bella giggled. "That's funny. My mom says I think so much I sometimes forget to talk."

"Really?" Abby grinned. "Maybe it's a good thing we became friends. We balance each other out!" She shot the other girl a questioning look. "We *are* friends, right?"

"Yes," Bella said without hesitation. "We're definitely friends. And we might be opposites, but at least we have one thing in common—dolphins!"

"Yeah!" Abby cheered. She peered out at the moonlit lagoon. "Hey, speaking of dolphins . . ."

Bella turned to look, too. Then she gasped. "It's them!" she said. "I think it's our pod!"

Abby just nodded, watching as several sleek gray

shapes leaped and played in the clear water. She was pretty sure she recognized Rascal, Graygirl, Domino . . .

"Maybe they came to check on Bogart," Bella said.

"Maybe." Impulsively, Abby reached over to give her new friend a hug. "Or maybe they're just excited to be a part of Dolphin Island Family Resort—like us!"

Read on to discover how the adventures
at Dolphin Island continues!

# Lost in the Storm

Abby Feingold stepped out of the woods into the sheltered cove. The water was calm, ruffled only slightly by the breeze coming off the ocean.

"Anybody here?" Abby called. She took another step toward the rocky shore's edge. "Dolphins? Yoo-hoo!"

She let out a loud whistle. A second later, a sleek gray head popped into view.

Abby smiled. "Rascal!" she called. "I'm glad the weather report didn't scare you away."

A gust of wind blew her wavy brown hair into her

face. Abby pushed it back, squinting out at the dolphin. He was bobbing in the water, watching her with his big, dark eyes. Where were the others?

She got her answer a moment later when five more dolphins popped into sight. One of them, Echo, leaped up and dove back into the water with a splash.

Abby laughed. "Do it again," she called, pulling her phone out of her pocket. "I told Daddy and Rachel I'd take some photos for the resort's website."

Abby lived on Barnaby Key, a small island in the Florida Keys. The island had been a wedding gift from a relative to her father and brand-new stepmother. Now Abby, Daddy, and Rachel lived there full-time and ran Dolphin Island Family Resort. The resort had only been open for a month, but Abby already couldn't imagine living anywhere else! She especially loved the cove, and the pod of dolphins that came there every day. She and her friend Bella had named all of the dolphins: Rascal, Echo, Domino, Graygirl, Nana, and Neptune.

Abby snapped some photos of the dolphins playing. They dove and jumped, doing flips and twists in the air or skimming along just below the surface. She laughed as Neptune did a loud belly flop. Just then another gust of wind almost blew the phone out of her hand.

"Wow," she said to Graygirl, who was floating near the shore. "I guess the hurricane must be getting closer."

She frowned, a little worried. She wasn't afraid of hurricanes—as a lifelong Florida girl, she had been through several. But she wasn't sure how a hurricane would affect the island and its wildlife, including the dolphins.

Then she shrugged off her worries. "Oh well," she murmured. "The forecasters don't even know if the storm is coming toward us or not."

Just then the phone buzzed in her hand. It was a text from Rachel:

*Guests heading out soon—come back if u want to say bye!*

"Oops." Abby realized she'd lost track of the time. That happened a lot when she was at the cove! "Sorry, guys," she called to the dolphins. "I have to go."

Echo let out a soft whistle, as if he understood what she had said. Abby smiled and whistled back. Then she turned and hurried into the woods, following the familiar trail among the palm, gumbo limbo, and buttonwood trees.

A few minutes later, she emerged into a large open area. At the center stood the main house. Six guest bungalows were scattered across the beautiful grounds. Daddy had worked as a landscaper back on the mainland, and he still loved getting his hands dirty planting all sorts of beautiful flowers, vines, and shrubs.

The house faced a sheltered lagoon with crystal-blue water and a white sand beach. At one end of the beach was the dock where Abby's family kept their motorboat, the *Kismet*. Daddy and Rachel used the boat to take guests back and forth between the resort and Key West, a large, busy island with an airport and lots of shops and restaurants, which was about three miles away.

At the moment, Daddy was fiddling with the ropes tying the boat to the pilings. The departing guests were waiting to board. Some stood on the dock with their suitcases, while others were taking a few final photos on the beach or beneath the majestic palms.

Rachel and some of the resort employees were there, too, chatting with the guests or helping with the luggage. Abby also spotted Carlos Alvarez, the eight-year-old nephew of Sofia, the resort's head cook. Occasionally Carlos took the boat out with her from Key West, where they both lived, and spent the day on Barnaby Key.

"Hey, Carlos," Abby said, hurrying over. "Are you leaving already? I was hoping you could help us clean up everything before next week's guests get here."

Carlos tossed his dark hair out of his eyes. "I can't, sorry," he said, though he didn't sound very sorry. "I'm going back with your dad right now—I have soccer practice this afternoon."

"Oh, okay," Abby said. Then she laughed as a bright-eyed two-year-old toddled toward them, clutching a seashell in one hand. "Bye-bye, Tandi," Abby said, scooping up the girl to give her a hug. "We'll miss you!"

The girl's mother stepped forward, smiling. "Don't worry, Abby," she said. "I'm sure we'll be back soon. We had such a lovely time here!"

"Yes." The woman's husband joined them, dragging a large suitcase. He squinted at the horizon, where a few ragged gray clouds marred the blue sky. "But don't expect us next week—we're from Chicago, you know. We don't do hurricanes!"

# Don't miss any of the

# Dolphin
## ❧ School ❧
## books!

#1: Pearl's Ocean Magic

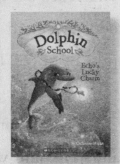

#2: Echo's Lucky Charm

#3: Splash's Secret Friend

#4: Flip's Surprise Talent

#5: Echo's New Pet

#6: Pearl's Perfect Gift

#7: Flip's Great Escape

#8: Splash's Big Heart

# THE PUPPY PLACE

# READ THEM ALL!

- ❏ Angel
- ❏ Bandit
- ❏ Barney
- ❏ Baxter
- ❏ Bear
- ❏ Bella
- ❏ Bentley
- ❏ Bitsy
- ❏ Bonita
- ❏ Boomer
- ❏ Bubbles and Boo
- ❏ Buddy
- ❏ Champ
- ❏ Chewy and Chica

- ❏ Cocoa
- ❏ Cody
- ❏ Cooper
- ❏ Daisy
- ❏ Edward
- ❏ Flash
- ❏ Gizmo
- ❏ Goldie
- ❏ Gus
- ❏ Honey
- ❏ Jack
- ❏ Jake
- ❏ Kodiak
- ❏ Liberty
- ❏ Lola
- ❏ Louie

- ❏ Lucky
- ❏ Lucy
- ❏ Maggie and Max
- ❏ Mocha
- ❏ Molly
- ❏ Moose
- ❏ Muttley
- ❏ Nala
- ❏ Noodle
- ❏ Oscar
- ❏ Patches
- ❏ Princess
- ❏ Pugsley
- ❏ Rascal
- ❏ Rocky

- ❏ Roxy
- ❏ Rusty
- ❏ Scout
- ❏ Shadow
- ❏ Snowball
- ❏ Spirit
- ❏ Stella
- ❏ Sugar, Gummi, and Lollipop
- ❏ Sweetie
- ❏ Teddy
- ❏ Winnie
- ❏ Ziggy
- ❏ Zipper

## 📖 SCHOLASTIC

scholastic.com

PUPPYPLACE57

# MEET RANGER

## A time-traveling golden retriever with search-and-rescue training . . . and a nose for danger!